Hide-and-Seek Duck

Story and Pictures by
CYNDY SZEKERES

A GOLDEN BOOK • NEW YORK

Western Publishing Company, Inc., Racine, Wisconsin 53404

Duck is playing hide-and-seek.
He is looking for Little Bunny.

3

Duck looks on top of a tree stump.

4

Owl is there, fluffing his feathers.
But there is no Little Bunny.

5

Duck looks under a berry bush.
Frog is there, singing, "Garump, guddy-rump!"
But there is no Little Bunny.

7

Duck looks high up in a pine tree.
Squirrel is there, crunch-munching nuts.
But there is no Little Bunny.

8

Duck looks inside a mossy tunnel.
Ssh! Chipmunk is there, taking a nap.
But there is no Little Bunny.

11

Duck looks down.
There are two furry paws behind his own feet!

"Boo!" laughs Little Bunny.
Duck catches him with a hug.

Now it is Duck's turn to hide!

14

15